SkippyjonJones

LOST IN SPICE

JUDY SCHACHNER

• DUTTON CHILDREN'S BOOKS •

To my great-nieces, Miranda and Ella

Love,
Judy

DUTTON CHILDREN'S BOOKS
A division of Penguin Young Readers Group

PUBLISHED BY THE PENGUIN GROUP

Penguin Group (USA) Inc., 375 Hudson Street, New York, New York 10014, U.S.A. • Penguin Group (Canada), 90 Eglinton Avenue East, Suite 700, Toronto, Ontario M4P 2Y3, Canada (a division of Pearson Penguin Canada Inc.) • Penguin Books Ltd, 80 Strand, London WC2R 0RL, England • Penguin Ireland, 25 St Stephen's Green, Dublin 2, Ireland (a division of Penguin Books Ltd) • Penguin Group (Australia), 250 Camberwell Road, Camberwell, Victoria 3124, Australia (a division of Pearson Australia Group Pty Ltd) • Penguin Books India Pvt Ltd, 11 Community Centre, Panchsheel Park, New Delhi - 110 017, India • Penguin Group (NZ), 67 Apollo Drive, Rosedale, North Shore 0632, New Zealand (a division of Pearson New Zealand Ltd) • Penguin Books (South Africa) (Pty) Ltd, 24 Sturdee Avenue, Rosebank, Johannesburg 2196, South Africa • Penguin Books Ltd, Registered Offices: 80 Strand, London WC2R 0RL, England

Library of Congress Cataloging-in-Publication Data
Schachner, Judith Byron. Skippyjon Jones, lost in spice / Judy Schachner. p. cm.
Summary: Skippyjon Jones, the Siamese cat that thinks he is a Chihuahua dog, has an adventure on Mars. ISBN 978-0-525-47965-9 [1. Siamese cat—Fiction. 2. Cats—Fiction. 3. Chihuahua (Dog breed)—Fiction. 4. Dogs—Fiction. 5. Interplanetary voyages—Fiction. 6. Mars (Planet)—Fiction.] I. Title. PZ7.S3286Ske 2009 [E]—dc22 2008048978

Published in the United States by Dutton Children's Books,
a division of Penguin Young Readers Group, 345 Hudson Street, New York, New York 10014
www.penguin.com/youngreaders

Designed by Heather Wood

Printed in U.S.A. • First Edition • 10 9 8 7 6 5 4 3

The illustrations for this book were created in acrylics and pen and ink on Aquarelle Arches watercolor paper.

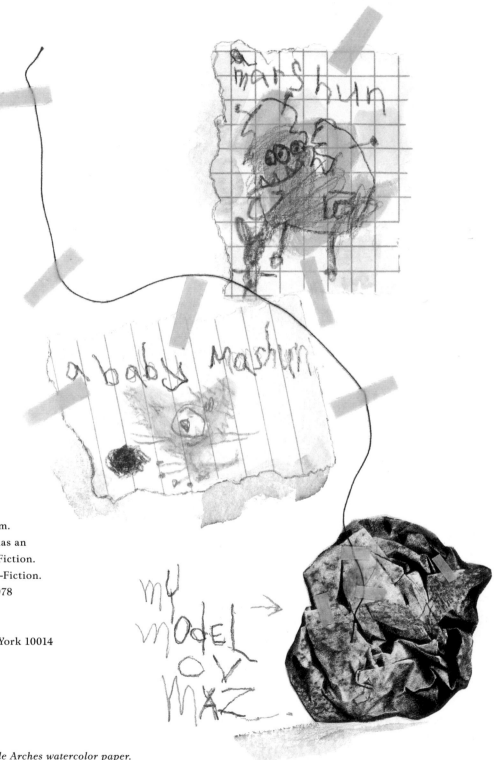

Skippyjon Jones was
nuts about Mars . . .

Because it was the RED planet.

"I love RED,
   That's what I said,
   And I must-y put some rust-y
   In my big-boy bed!"

So off he went to the kitchen where
Mama and the girls were starting supper.

"We're making Tuna Poodle casserole," crooned his sister Jilly Boo Jones.

"Tuna *Noodle* casserole," corrected Mama. "A poodle is a dog, and we don't eat dogs."

"Skippyjon thinks he's a dog," said Jezebel.

"Yeah," agreed Ju-Ju Bee. "He thinks he's a *chi-wow-wow.*"

"Because his ears are too big for his head," added Jezebel.

"That's enough," scolded Mama. "Pinky Pie's ears are just fine."

But Pinky Pie was oblivious to their chatter.

"May I please borrow your bottles of red spice, Mama?" he asked politely.

"Yes, you may," replied Mama, pleased with her boy's manners. "But you better not be *thinking* of doing any **sprinkling**."

"Nuh-uh," said Skippy, blinking.

"Or *tasting,*

pasting,

or

wasting...

"If you know what is good for you," she added.

Well, Skippyjon Jones always knew what was good for him.

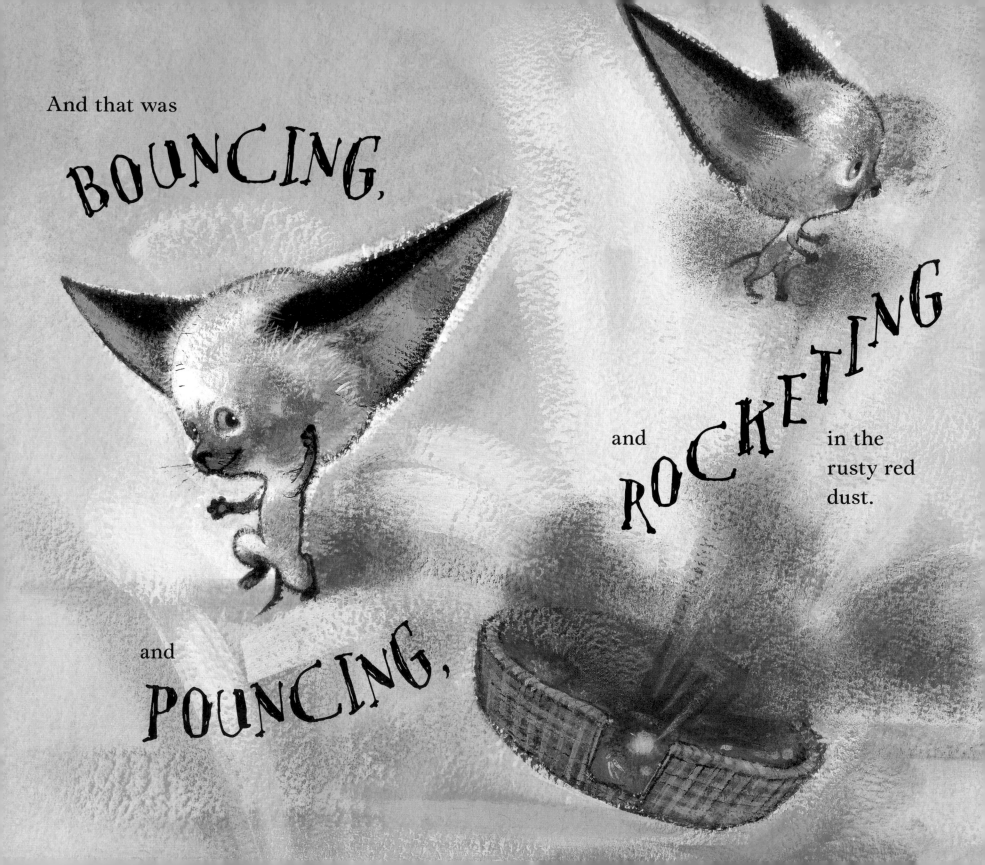

And that was

BOUNCING,

and

POUNCING,

and ROCKETING in the rusty red dust.

"Oh, I'm **SkippyjonJones**,
And I'm in a big race
To be the first dog
To bounce into space."

Then a bit of the spice
tickled his nose and . . .

"aaaah-cah-
CHOOey!"

The kitty boy sneezed.

"Holy **HOT** tamales!" exclaimed Skippyjon Jones as he shot past his reflection.

"What's up with that doggie in the mirror?"

Then using his very best Spanish accent, he said, "You are not a Siamese cat, dude. You are a weeck-ed **RED Chihuahua!**"

And quicker than you can say "jumping jacks on Jupiter," the kitty boy found his mask and cape, a mirror, a marble, and his sock monkey.

He stuffed these and a few other things into his space suit while he sang in a *muy muy* soft voice:

"My name is Skippito Friskito, (clap-clap)

And I think there are Martian perritos.

(clap-clap)

Some say the green creatures

Share all of my features

I hope it's not just fable-itos." (clap-clap)

Back in the kitchen, the girls were being a big help to Mama Junebug Jones.

"I love noodles," declared Jilly Boo.

"Noodles are silly," said Jezebel.

"That's because they're NOOD," said Ju-Ju Bee.

"They're not nude," said Jilly Boo, giggling. "They're naked!" And she tossed one up to the ceiling, where it stuck.

But Skippyjon Jones wasn't stuck at all. He was
suited up and ready for liftoff. The astronaut-ito took
one small step into his closet for Chihuahuas . . .

. . .and one giant leap into the universe for Los Chimichangos. He was well into his orbit when a comet covered in crazies cruised by.

"Who goes there?" hollered Skippito.

"Martian," came the answer.

"Martian Who?"

"Martian to your closet and get us some *frijoles*, dude," said the voice.

"Poquito Tito!" exclaimed Skippito. "Is that you, *amigo*?"

"*Sí*, it is all of us, Los Chimichangos," said Poquito Tito, the smallest of the small ones. "We are going to build a chili *polvo* pipeline from Mars to Earth, puppito."

"Not the chili powder pipeline," declared Skippito.

"*¡Exactamente!*" howled the doggies.

"*¿Por qué?*" asked Skippito.

"Because, *amigo*," began Don Diego, the biggest of the small ones, "the chili powder on Mars is *muy caliente* and it will keep us very warm *en el invierno*."

Then off they zoomed.

The cuckoo comet and the kitty boy made it to
Mars with a soft landing.

"Oooooo," sighed Don Diego. "That felt
marvelous!"

Then he turned to glance at Skippito.

"No offense, *poco coco*, but
why the suit *de la nieve*?"
asked Don Diego.

"It's not a SNOW suit,"
declared Skippito.
"It's a SPACE suit."

"Dude, you don't need a space suit up here,"
said Poquito Tito. "You need a SPICE suit.
Mars is covered in the chili powder, *chico*!"

This made the *perros* go *loco* in the *rojo* singing:

"Chili-roo, chili-ree, chili-rito, (clap-clap)

It's a wag of the tail for Skippito.

(clap-clap) For there's nothing as nice

As a roll in hot spice

In the light of the Martian moon-itos."

(clap-clap)

But a roll in the *rojo* should have been a no-no because quicker than you can say "monkeys making meatballs," Skippito rolled and rolled and rolled in the opposite direction from his pipeline poochitos.

SPICE ZONE 2 MPH

"Whew!" said Skippito, panting. "You boys are right. The spice-ito is HOT!" The astronaut-ito was so *calor* under the collar that he just had to take off his space suit.

"Mooo-chaaaaaaaaa-Chos!"

he called out.
There was no answer.

"Uh-oh," Skippito said to himself.
"I'm lost in spice."

But the astronaut-ito did not
panic. He grabbed his binoculars
and climbed up onto a *roca*. And
that's when he saw it . . .

"Holy green
gorillas,"
gulped Skippito.
"It's a Martian-ito!"

The poochito pounced just
a whisker away from the
unearthly creature.

"Dude."

"Dude."

"Your ears are
too big for your head."

"Your ears are
too big for your head."

"Your head is
too big for your body."

"Your head is
too big for your body."

"You are not a Martian."

"You are not a Martian."

"No, I know I'm not a Martian, dude," said Skippito. "I am a Chihuahua. Just like you!"

To prove his point, Skippito ran back to his space suit and pulled out the little *rojo* mirror he had packed.

"Look!" said Skippito, holding it up so both their faces showed. "We are tweens!"

The Martian was so mesmerized that he could not take his *uno ojo* off himself. Skippito was so excited that he could not stop hopping and flapping his arms. Then all of a sudden he remembered that he was lost.

"Hey, c'mon, Uno Ojo," called the kitty boy. "We've got to find *mis amigos*."

But Uno Ojo said *nada*. He simply sat and stared at his image in the mirror.

"Okey-doke-ito," said Skippito. "I'll go. But you have to keep your eye on my stuff, especially my sock monkey."

Then he took off faster than a tiddly-wink in a tornado.

He didn't have to go far. In less time than it takes
to tickle a termite, Skippito found his cuckoo-ritos
cooped up inside a crater.

"Dudes!"
shouted Skippito.

"Dude," whispered Don Diego.
"You are just in *tiempo*."
"In time for what?" Skippito
asked.

"*Hombres de la Marte*," said
Poquito Tito with a shiver-ito.
"Not the men from Mars!"
declared Skippito.

The mere mention of Martians made the *muchachos* go mad.

"Knock, knock. Who goes there?

Verde Martians everywhere!

Slurping sloppy ice-green cones,

Speeding in the spicy zones.

Mossy Martians on the move,

What do they think they have to prove?

We did not come here for a fight.

We want to build, we will not bite!"

Then Skippito felt the fur stand up on the back of his neck.

Because the critters' crater was about to have *cinco* crazy creatures for company.

"Holy Hoopleheads!" hollered Skippito. "Here they come!"

Before Skippito could think what to do, the *verde* visitors piled out of their space buggy bearing all of Skippito's stuff.

Two were green and mossy,

while the third was green and bossy.

The fourth was green and funky,

and the fifth was green and . . .

"MONKEY!" yelled Skippito. "That's my sock monkey!"

"Ditto!" declared Skippito's one-eyed Martian twin emerging from the green group before him.

Without saying another *palabra*, Skippito picked up his monkey's paw and pulled.

First Skippito yanked it **THIS** way.

Then Uno Ojo yanked it **THAT** way.

"It's tug-o-monk-ito!" cheered the Chimichangos. On the count of three the puppitos planned to pull *también*. But as the doggies shouted,

"*UNO!*"

the Martians hollered,

"*Ojo!*"

And
UH-OH!
Uno Ojo let-a-go-go, sending the kitty boy flying.

Skippito and his sock monkey hurtled headfirst back to Earth and out through his closet door.

"KA-BOOM!" he hollered, breaking the sound barrier and maybe his head.

"Skippyjon Jones!" exclaimed Mama, rushing into his room. "What on Earth are you doing?"

The kitty boy stood up and shook off a cloud of red spice.

"I didn't do anything on Earth, Mama," replied Skippyjon. "I did everything on Mars."

"Oh, that's terrific, Major Tom," said Mama. Then she straightened the kitty boy's ears. "You must be starving."

Later that night, the kitty boy looked up at the starry sky.

"Mars," he muttered, beginning to bounce.

"Oh, I'm SkippyjonJones,

and I like my red jammies,

'cuz they're made from the wool

of green Martian lambies."

"Stop bouncing, Pinky Pie," scolded Mama.

"I'm not pink, I'm red," said Skippy.

"It's over, Red Rover," said Mama. "Just go to sleep."

And that's exactly what he did.